JACK AND THE WIZARD
Magical Stories from Around the World

About John Matthews

John Matthews is an historian, folklorist and author. He has been a full time writer since 1980 and has produced over ninety books on the Arthurian Legends and Grail Studies, as well as short stories and a volume of poetry. He has devoted much of the past thirty years to the study of Arthurian Traditions and myth in general. His best known and most widely read works are 'Pirates' (Carlton/Atheneum), No 1 children's book on the New York Times Review best-seller list for 22 weeks in 2006, 'The Grail, Quest for Eternal Life' (Thames & Hudson, 1981) 'The Encyclopaedia of Celtic Wisdom' (Element, 1994) and 'The Winter Solstice' (Quest Books, 1999) which won the Benjamin Franklin Award for that year. His book 'Celtic Warrior Chiefs' was a New York Public Library recommended title for young people.

John has been involved in a number of media projects, as an advisor and contributor, including an animated Arthurian TV series, a film about the magical defense of Britain during the 2nd World War, and "The Real Merlin" for Channel 4 UK. In 2003, he was the historical advisor to the Jerry Bruckheimer movie, "King Arthur", and has made appearances on both History Channel and Discovery Channel specials on Arthur and the Holy Grail.

Much in demand as a speaker both in Europe and the USA, he has taught at (among others) the Temenos Academy in London, St Hilda's College, Oxford, and at the New York Open Centre, The Omega Centre, and the University of Seattle in Washington. He has also worked in collaboration with the Joseph Campbell Foundation and The Lorian Association, with whom he continues to retain contact. Despite other commitments, he manages to find time to continue his studies and is working on several new projects, including a series of Graphic novels on King Arthur and a top-secret project about faeries. He has just recently sold his first movie script and is currently developing several others. He is married to the writer, Caitlín Matthews. The Matthews live in Oxford, England.

JACK AND THE WIZARD

Magical Stories from Around the World

Retold by
John Matthews

Starseed Books
2016

Jack and the Wizard:
Magical Stories from Around the World

Edited by Aidan Spangler
Cover and Interior Art by Deva Berg
Book Design by Jeremy Berg

Starseed Books
6592 Peninsula Dr
Traverse City, MI 49686

ISBN: 978-1-939790-10-1

Matthews, John
Jack and the Wizard: Magical Stories from Around the World/
John Matthews

Library of Congress Control Number: 2016941280

First Edition: May 2016

CONTENTS

INTRODUCTION

Some of these tales, in a slightly different form, appeared in the collection *The Wizard King and Other Stories*. Others are new to the collection and the frame story was written especially for this edition. I would like to thank all at Starseed Books for taking this on, especially Deva Berg for her inspired illustrations, Aidan Spangler for his insight, Jeremy Berg for his design skills, and my friend David Spangler for suggesting the ending.

John Matthews
Oxford, 2015

JACK AND THE WIZARD

Jack had always wanted to be a Wizard. Everyone else, including his parents, told him he was mad. Then one day he heard that the great Wizard Sidesaddle, who lived on the hill overlooking the valley where Jack lived, was looking for an apprentice. Of course everyone said it was the most foolish thing he had ever done—and he had done a few foolish things in his time—but Jack set out at once for the Wizard's house.

It was a long walk, and mostly uphill, but Jack ran most of the way. He could not contain his excitement. "I'm going to be a Wizard," he told himself, as he climbed the long, steep path to the Wizard's house.

The closer he got the bigger and more forbidding the house looked. It had several tall towers that looked as if they were wearing pointed hats, and a lot of strange-shaped windows that reminded Jack of eyes.

When at last he stood in front of the door he wasn't quite so sure about being a Wizard. The door was big and dark and forbidding, and the knocker—which was very high up—was carved in the shape of an odd-looking face with leaves sprouting out of its mouth and nose and ears.

Just as Jack was summoning up all his courage, the door flew open and a strange man, who was not much taller than Jack, looked out.

"There you are," he said, "I've been waiting for you all day."

Jack stared at the small man in astonishment. He had a large head and a very long nose, on the tip of which were perched a pair of old fashioned glasses. Behind them his eyes were very sharp indeed and Jack had the uncomfortable feeling that he was being looked at all the way through his skin and bones.

"I.... came about...." he began.

"Yes, yes, the job." said the strange man. "Come in, we haven't got all day."

He opened the door wider and beckoned Jack to follow him.

Inside, the house was big and dark and scary. As his eyes grew accustomed to the gloom Jack found himself standing in a huge hall with stairs leading upward in the darkness on either side. But the strangest thing about it was that it was full of green and growing things.

Jack was used to seeing houses covered in creeper on the outside, but the Wizard's house seemed to have everything backwards. In the hall, a huge tree grew out of the middle of the floor, its branches twining round the stairway and the banisters. Huge creepers covered the walls and hung down from the ceiling. There was a strong earthy smell everywhere.

"Come along, come along, we haven't got all day," said the little man again.

Jack followed him through a door on the right side of the hall and found himself in a room with a big log-fire blazing in the hearth. Sunlight came in through two big windows. Everywhere there were heaps of scrolls with strange writing on them, and other objects that Jack couldn't even begin to think what they might be for.

Suddenly the place looked a lot friendlier.

The little man sat down in a big armchair and motioned Jack to join him. He perched on a little three-legged stool and looked at his host.

"Are you...."

"Sidesaddle," answered the Wizard. "And you are Jack. Yes, I know all about you and of course the job is yours." He paused. "I expect you'd like to know what your duties are?"

Jack nodded, too amazed that the Wizard knew about him to

speak. "Let me see," said Sidesaddle, "There are potions to mix, spells to copy out, crystal balls to polish, dragon's eggs to hatch..."

Suddenly Jack decided he liked the Wizard.

"Will I learn magic?" he asked

"Of course. Eventually." answered Sidesaddle. "But first, you have to learn what it means to be a Wizard."

"How shall I do that?" asked Jack.

"By watching and listening of course," answered Sidesaddle. "If you do your work well I shall tell you a story every second Tuesday and Saturday."

So that was how Jack became the apprentice to the Wizard Sidesaddle. He slept in a little room half way up one of the towers from which he could see his home.

His new master turned out to be kind as well as wise. Every day Jack worked hard at mixing potions, polishing the seven great crystal balls and hatching dragon's eggs.

And every second Tuesday and Saturday, just as he had promised, Sidesaddle told him another story about many different kinds of Wizard: young wizards, old wizards, clever wizards and even bad wizards. And slowly, without even noticing at first, Jack began to understand just what it did mean to be a Wizard.

THE STORY OF EMRYS

(A Story from Wales)

"So how do you get to be a wizard?" asked Jack one Tuesday. "I mean, I know I'm your apprentice—but what if there's no one around to teach you?"

"That's a good question," said Sidesaddle. Some people say that Wizards are born and that no one can teach you how to be one. Others say that it's all a matter of learning the right incantations and spells. Let me tell you the story of one of the greatest Wizards who ever lived, and maybe you'll see what I mean."

***************************   ************************

It all began with dragons.

Long ago in Britain there lived a king named Vortigern. He was not a good man, and no one really liked him. In fact, they said that he had stolen the crown, and that the real king was named Ambrosias the Golden. But no one knew where he was—until one day a huge army showed up off the shores of Britain, and its leader, who said that he was Ambrosius, told everyone that he had come to claim back the kingdom.

When King Vortigern heard this he grew fearful. He summoned his Wizards and asked them what he should do.

"There is only one way to escape Ambrosius," said the Chief

5

Wizard . "You must build a new castle and stay in it until he goes away."

"Where shall I build this castle?" he asked.

The Chief Wizard thought for a moment. Then he pointed to a tall hill on the horizon.

"There," he said.

Vortigern sent for his builders and told them to make him a strong castle on top of the hill.

To begin with everything was fine. The builders dug huge foundations and dragged massive blocks of stone up the hillside. The walls began to grow upwards until they were nearly as tall as a tall man. And then .... during the night .... they fell down.

In the morning the builders came to admire their work, and the great stone blocks were rolled about all over the hillside like giant square marbles.

"Earthquake," said the head builder. "That's what it was. You'll see."

So they set about building the walls again, and by nightfall they were back in place. Then the builders went off to bed, satisfied they had done a good job.

But.

Next morning the stones were scattered all over the hillside again. And this time the earth was all dug up around them as though someone with very large feet had walked about, kicking the stones.

Now the builders were really worried. So they sent a message to King Vortigern.

When he heard what had happened, he sent for his Wizards.

"Ah'" said the Chief Wizard, stroking his long white beard

and looking wise. "It's obvious that some evil spirit is at work here. It must be knocking down the walls every night."

"What shall I do?"he said.

"Well," answered the Chief Wizard, "You must find a boy who has no father. And when you find him you must kill him and sprinkle his blood on the stones. That will do it."

Vortigern sent for the Captain of his soldiers and told him to go and look for a boy without a father, and to be quick about it, because Ambrosius and his army were getting closer, and Vortigern needed to have his new castle finished as soon as possible.

The Captain gathered his best men and told them to ride North, South, East, and West and every direction in between, until they found a boy without a father.

In the end, it was the Captain himself who found the boy.

He was riding through a little town not far from the hill where Vortigern was trying to build his castle, when he saw some boys fighting. One of the boys broke away from the rest and ran off. As he did so, the others shouted after him:

"Emrys has no father! Emrys has no father!"

At once the Captain rode after the boy. When he caught up with him he called out, "Boy! Wait! Is it true? Do you really have no father?"

The boy stopped and looked up at the Captain on his tall horse.

He had one blue eye and one green.

He nodded.

"Then you must come with me," said the Captain.

"I will," said the boy, and climbed up in front of the Captain.

He said nothing at all on the way to the hill. When they arrived they found that Vortigern himself, and his Wizards, were already there.

"Is this the boy?" demanded the king.

"It is," said the Captain, saluting.

Vortigern looked at the boy.

"What is your name?" he asked.

"Emrys," said the boy.

Vortigern looked at his wizards, who nodded.

"Proceed," said the King.

"I know you want to kill me," said the boy called Emrys, "But I know the real reason why your castle will not stand."

"What's that?" said Vortigern.

"There is a lake of water under the hill," said the boy. "Under the water there is a stone chest with a lid." He looked at Vortigern's Wizards. "Do you know what is inside the chest?" he asked.

The Wizards scratched their heads and tugged at their beards and shifted from one foot to the other. But not one of them said anything.

"Well?" said Vortigern.

"Inside the chest are two dragons," said the boy. "Every night they come out and fight in the lake. Their fighting shakes the earth and makes the walls of your castle fall down. If you don't believe me, tell your builders to dig down into the hill."

Vortigern gave the order, and the builders began to dig. The hole got deeper and deeper until they revealed a lake of still, dark water. Then they brought pumps and engines and began to drain the lake. Soon the water was almost gone, and everyone

8

could see the top of a huge stone chest.

Vortigern's builders brought a crane and some ropes and slowly, slowly they lifted off the lid.

Inside, curled up, sleeping, were two dragons.

One was red and the other white.

They woke up.

They crawled out of the stone chest and stretched their wings.

King Vortigern and his Wizards and all the builders and soldiers drew back in fear.

The boy did not move.

Then the two dragons flew up into the air and began to fight with each other.

The noise was like thunder and lightning and wind all at once.

At last the white dragon began to grow tired.

The red dragon bit it on the neck. Then it breathed out some fire.

The white dragon fell dead.

You could hear the crash a hundred leagues away.

The red dragon flew away.

Everyone was very silent on the hillside. King Vortigern looked at the boy.

"How did you know about the dragons?" he asked.

"I know many things," answered the boy. "I know that King Ambrosius the Golden is coming with a great army, and that he will soon be here. And I know that you are going be killed, just like the white dragon."

With that the boy vanished, leaving the king and his wizards and all his men very much afraid.

And everything the boy had said would happen did happen. King Ambrosius came with his army and Vortigern was killed in the battle that followed.

His castle never did get finished. In fact, you can still see the ruins today, if you can find the hill.

As to the boy named Emrys, he grew up to become the greatest wizard that ever lived. But he was not called Emrys any longer. Everyone called him Merlin, and he was King Arthur's magician. And everyone said he was the wisest man who ever lived.

****

"I wish I could do things like that," said Jack. "Do you think I might, if I keep up my studies?"

"It's entirely possible," said Sidesaddle. "But there could only ever be one Merlin, and he was born magic."

"Did you know him?" asked Jack.

"O yes," said Sidesaddle. "In fact, he was my teacher."

"So if I become a proper wizard I could say that I studied with the Wizard who was taught by the Greatest Wizard that ever lived!"

"Hmmm," said Sidesaddle. "I suppose you could. But first you'll have to learn how to make really good mashed potatoes.

"Mashed potatoes?" said Jack, confusedly.

"It's what I want for supper," said his master. "I suggest you go and get on with it!"

THE WIZARD WHO GOT SICK

(A story from Armenia)

One day Jack woke up with a cold. He could not stop sneezing and snorting and dripping and wheezing until finally Sidesaddle snapped his fingers and the cold went away.

"Thank you," said Jack. "It must be nice to be a wizard and never get sick."

Sidesaddle stopped powdering unicorn's horn and looked at him. "I knew a wizard who got very sick," he said.

"Please tell me," said Jack.

"Well, I suppose you could learn something from it," answered his Master. He put the bowl of freshly powdered horn to one side, where it continued to sparkle for some time.

**************************  **************************

There was once a wizard who grew sick. Every medicine he tried made him feel worse, and so he consulted his magic books. There he found it written that travel might be good for him. And so he decided to go out and wander the world until he felt better.

On the first day, he came to where a fountain of fresh water bubbled up out of the earth. A number of women from a nearby village were filling their water jars and washing their clothes in the fountain.

The wizard walked up to the women and asked if he could have some of the water to drink

"Not if you turned to dust before my eyes," said one woman. And the rest were all as rude and unfriendly. Except, that is, for one, who looked at the thirsty wizard and said, "We can spare a drop of water for a poor man."

As the wizard drank deeply she said, "There is a corner of our barn ready for you if you'd like to sleep there tonight."

The wizard thanked her for her kindness and went home with her.

The woman's husband met them at the door.

"Who is this you have brought home?" he asked.

"A stranger' said the woman,"and our guest this night."

"Then come in and be welcome' said the man. "I will set the table."

"I'm afraid I only eat freshly killed beef," said the wizard, who had noticed that they had a single cow tied up next to their house.

"Then I shall go and kill the cow," said the man without hesitation. "Only the best is good enough for a guest."

That evening they all ate well, and the wizard went off to sleep in the barn. As he left the house he heard the woman saying quietly to her husband that she did not know how they would manage now that the cow was gone.

Next morning the couple were woken by the sound of a cow lowing outside.

"What can that be?" asked the woman.

"I don't know," said the man. "We only had one cow and we ate that last night."

THE WIZARD WHO GOT SICK

They went outside and there, to their amazement, was their own cow, hale and hearty as ever and very much alive.

But of their guest there was no sign.

Meanwhile, the wizard went on his way, and as the sun rose high in the sky he met a man gathering brushwood.

"Ho, brother, you won't grow fat that way." said the wizard.

"What more can I do," answered the man. "There's no other work for me."

The wizard waved a hand and the dry twigs and branches became a thriving vineyard full of ripe grapes ready for picking and making into wine.

"May you prosper brother, "said the wizard, and he went on his way.

Further along the road he saw a man walking sadly among a grove of dead trees.

"Hey, that's a fine orchard you have there!" cried the wizard.

And sure enough the trees were suddenly heavy with fruit.

"Prosper and be well, brother," said the wizard, and leaving the astonished man, he went on his way.

Next he saw a man carrying rocks on his back.

"That's a fine herd of sheep you have there my friend' said the wizard.

At once all the rocks turned into fat sheep.

"May you prosper always," cried the wizard, and went on his way.

For a whole year he travelled about doing deeds of this kind, until he was completely cured of his sickness. Then he decided to return the way he had come and see how the people he had helped were faring.

First, he came back to the man whose stones he had turned into sheep.

The man had slaughtered all the beasts and was having a huge feast.

"Can you spare some of that delicious looking meat for me?" asked the wizard.

"Be off with you' shouted the man. "Did you help me look after the sheep?"

"Give me at least a morsel, for the sake of charity," said the wizard.

But the man only shouted at him to go away.

The wizard waved his hands and the roasting sheep turned back into stones.

Then he went on his way until he came to the apple orchard, where men were busy picking fruit.

"May I have an apple?" asked the wizard.

"Clear off!," shouted the owner of the orchard, "We don't want your sort here."

The wizard gestured with both hands and the trees became as barren as they had been before he had caused them to flower and bear fruit.

The wizard went on his way again, until he came to the vineyard.

"May I have some of your grapes?" he asked one of the workers.

"I'll ask the master," said the man.

He soon came back, shaking his head. "The master says you can drop dead before he'll give you a single grape."

THE WIZARD WHO GOT SICK

The wizard raised a hand and the vineyard vanished. A bundle of dead twigs lay on the ground in its place.

Again the wizard went on until he came to the house where the man and woman lived who had killed their only cow to feed him.

The couple came to the door, smiling and happy to see him.

"How good it is to see you again," said the man. "May we offer you something to tide you in your way." said the woman.

The wizard smiled.

"Truly you are good people." he said. "For all the good you have done and your kindness to me I will reward you. Every morning you shall find four hundred gold coins under your bed. May you always prosper."

With these words he vanished.

The couple were very glad, and you may be sure they lived very happily after that time.

As for the wizard, he went home and lived on for many years. And whenever he felt sick or low in spirits he would go and visit the couple that had offered him such kindness, and they would sit and talk of the ways of the world until the fire went out in the hearth.

***********************   ***********************

"What a great story!" said Jack.

"Well, it shows that if you are kind you are likely to get rewarded," said Sidesaddle. "Though I did hear about a girl who was kind to someone because she knew she would get a reward – that didn't work out too well I seem to remember. In fact, I think she's still flying about somewhere," he said vaguely, and went back to powdering unicorn horn.

MAGIC

(A Story From Old Russia)

"I suppose you've had lots of apprentices?" said Jack one day when he was tired of trying to turn himself into a frog.

Sidesaddle looked up from the scroll he was reading, a faraway look in his eyes. "Well, there was that boy Thomas," he said. "And Gavin and Rollo and Peter and at least two other Jacks..."

"Wait," interrupted Jack. "There were more like me?"

"Well, not exactly like you," said Sidesaddle. "Every one was different. I seem to remember the last Jack didn't ask as many questions as you."

Jack fell silent at this and the wizard picked up his scroll and continued reading. But after a moment he looked up again. "I remember hearing about a wizard who had lots of apprentices, all at the same time. I believe it was twelve. Can't imagine how he managed...."

Jack waited eagerly until his master put the scroll aside and began the story.

***************************   ************************

There was once an old man and an old woman who had a son they loved very much. But they were very poor, so the old man decided to apprentice his son to a master. That way he could learn a trade and be able to make his way in the world and look after his parents, as they grew still older.

So the old man set out for the city with his son and tried to find him a master. But no matter how many he asked—bakers, wheelwrights, blacksmiths, barrel makers, tanners and weavers, he could find no one who would give his son a place. All of them wanted money and the old man had nothing to pay them.

And so the two returned home sadly, and the old man and the old woman wept loud and long. But their son, whose name was Ivan, told them to cheer up.

"For," he said, "we can try again tomorrow in another part of the city."

So the old man and the old woman dried their tears and the next day the old man set out again for the city, with Ivan by his side.

But no matter how many people the old man spoke to, no one wanted to apprentice his son.

Then, at the end of the day, as they were preparing to return home again, a tall well-dressed man came up to the old father and asked him why he looked so sad.

"I have been looking everywhere for someone who will take my lad as an apprentice, but no one wants to take him on without payment, and I have no money."

"Well," said the stranger, looking at Ivan, "give him to me. In three years I will teach him many wonderful things. But remember this: you must be at this very spot exactly three years from now—not a minute earlier or a minute later. Otherwise you will not get your son back."

The old man was so overjoyed that he forget to ask the stranger's name, or where he lived, or even what he would teach

Ivan. He gave his son over into the man's keeping and went home joyfully to tell his wife all about their good fortune.

But what he did not know was that the man to whom he had apprenticed his son was a wizard.

Three years passed quickly. By that time the old man had completely forgotten the day and the hour that he was supposed to be back in the city to collect his son. But one day, shortly before the end of the three years, a strange bird alighted on a mound of earth next to the old man's house, and turned into a handsome young man.

Of course it was Ivan, and he went into his parents' house and told them that the three years were up on the next day and that the old man must go to the city and be at a certain place at a certain time.

"But," he said, "there are some things you should know. I am not my master's only apprentice. There are eleven others, and he doesn't want to give any of us up. In fact, the others have been with him forever because when their parents came to claim them, they could not recognise their children at all. If you don't recognise me tomorrow I shall be forced to stay as well."

"I shall have no difficulty in recognising my own son," said the father.

"It will not be so easy as that," said Ivan. "You see, our master is really a wizard, and he will make us all look exactly alike. And what is more, he will put us into other shapes, to make it even harder."

"What shall I do then?" cried the old man.

"Listen to me and all shall be well' said Ivan. "First of all my master will show you twelve white doves. And every one will look exactly the same, feather for feather, as the next. And he will ask you which one is me. Watch carefully, because as the doves fly overhead I shall fly just a little bit higher than the rest. And so you will know it is me."

"I shall not forget," said the old man.

"But that is not the end of it," said Ivan. "For my master will next lead out twelve horses: every one the same from mane to tail. And he will ask you to show him which one is your son. Watch carefully, because I shall stamp my right foot twice as you go past, and so you will know that it is me."

"Be sure I shall remember that," said his father.

"There is more yet," said Ivan. "Next my master will bring out twelve youths, and every one of them will look just the same, as though they had one mother. Look very carefully at each one of them. You will see that on the right cheek of one of them is a fly. That one will be me."

"I will do as you say," promised the old man.

With that the youth went outside and struck the mound of earth with his right foot. At once he turned back into a bird and flew away.

Next day, the old man went into the city and at the appointed time he was waiting at the exact same spot where he had met the wizard three years ago. And there, sure enough, came the tall well-dressed man.

"Good day to you old man," he said. "I have taught your son many wonderful things, just as I promised. But if you want him back you must recognise him. If you do not, he will have to stay with me forever."

Then, just as Ivan had said he would, the wizard set free

twelve white doves, every one of them alike in every way.

"Now show me your son," said the wizard.

The old man looked and looked, and every one of the birds seemed exactly the same. Then he noticed that one of them was flying a little bit higher than all the rest.

"That is my son," he said.

The wizard looked angry.

"Very well," he said, and snapped his fingers. There, in place of the twelve white doves, were twelve identical horses, every one of them as handsome and high stepping as the other.

"Which one of these is your son?" asked the wizard.

The old man looked and looked. He walked up the line of horses, and he walked down. Then he saw that one of them stamped its right foot twice on the ground, and he went up to that one and touched its mane.

"This is my son," he said.

"Well, well, well," said the wizard, looking even more angry.

He snapped his fingers and in the place of the twelve horses stood twelve young men, dressed in fine silk and linen and every one of them as alike as though they had been born to the same mother.

"And which one of these is your son?"

The old man walked up the line and down the line. Then he walked down the line and up the line.

The wizard tapped his foot.

The old man peered closely at every identical face until he saw that one of them had a fly on his right cheek. He stopped in front of that youth.

"This is my son," he said.

The wizard stamped his foot and vanished in a flash of light and a curl of smoke. Eleven of the youths vanished too, leaving the old man standing in the road with his son by his side.

Joyfully they embraced and set off for home together.

They went home and lived a happy life together. With the magic he had learned from the wizard Ivan earned them some money. But it was still not much, and so one day the boy said to his father,"Listen. I'm going to turn myself into a bird. Take me to market and sell me for the best price you can get. But don't sell the cage I shall be in, or I won't be able to get back."

Then he stamped on the earth with his right foot and became a bird in a beautiful golden cage. The old man went to market and soon had a crowd of people who wanted to buy the bird.

Then the wizard appeared and offered more than anyone.

The old man agreed, but took the bird from its cage. The wizard scowled mightily at this, and wrapped the bird in his handkerchief. Then he went home and called to his lovely daughter.

"See what I have for you," he cried. "That rascal who used to be my apprentice."

The wizard's daughter, who had taken a liking to Ivan, came running.

"Where is he?" she asked.

But when the wizard unfolded his handkerchief the bird was nowhere to be found.

Next week as market day approached, Ivan said, "I am going to turn myself into a horse. Take me to the market and sell me for the best price you can get. But be sure you keep my bridle, because otherwise I shall not be able to get back."

Then he stamped on the earth with his right foot and in a flash there stood a great wild black horse with the most wonderful jewelled bridle.

The old man took him to market and soon a crowd gathered.

Some offered one thing and some another, but soon the wizard arrived and he offered the most.

The old man took the money and began to take off the horse's bridle.

"Wait," said the wizard. How shall I lead my horse without a bridle?"

The old man hesitated. But all the other horse-dealers began to shout that he could not sell a horse without a bridle. What could he do? He gave the bridle to the wizard.

Smiling, the wizard went home, leading the horse. He took it to his stable and tethered it so tightly that it could not even move its head to eat or drink.

The wizard went inside and called to his daughter.

"See what I have caught," he said.

"What is it? asked the girl.

"None other than that rascal who used to be my apprentice."

The girl went out to the stable to look. But when she saw the horse tied up so tightly she took pity on it and loosened the reins. At once the horse pulled free and galloped off.

The girl ran indoors, weeping.

"I'm sorry, father. The horse has run away."

The wizard gave a great cry and turned himself into a grey wolf. He ran as fast as the wind and faster yet after the horse, and soon he almost caught up with it.

The horse came to the bank of a river, and—quick as a flash—turned into a perch and swam off.

But the wizard turned himself into a great greedy pike with savage teeth and swam after it as fast as the wind and faster.

The perch swam and swam until it was exhausted. Then it came to the bank where some lovely maidens were washing clothes. The perch jumped out of the water and became a golden ring that rolled to the feet of one of the maidens.

The wizard took his own shape again and demanded the golden ring.

The maiden threw it on the ground and when it struck the earth it shattered. And instead of the ring were several grains of wheat.

The wizard laughed and tuned himself into a cockerel. He began to peck at the wheat.

Then one of the grains became a hawk, and it tore the cockerel into pieces.

And that was the end of the wizard.

As for Ivan, he went home and continued to make his old parents rich. And I did hear that he married the wizard's daughter, but whether that is true or not I cannot say.

**************************   ************************

"He wasn't a very nice wizard was he?" said Jack, when Sidesaddle had finished his story.

"Well not all of us are," answered his master. "Sometimes the fact that they can do magic leads them into bad ways. But you see how useful it was for Ivan to be able to turn himself into various creatures. How's that frog spell coming along?"

"I think it still needs a bit more work," said Jack, holding up one green hand with webbed fingers.

"Ah," said Sidesaddle, "I would give it a bit more energy."

THE MAGICIAN'S HORSE

(A Story from Greece)

One of Jack's regular duties was to clean out the stable where the wizard kept a great black horse. Generally he did this willingly enough, and whenever he could he brought an apple or some other piece of fruit to give to the horse.

But one day, Jack was tired and hot and had spent a long time trying to raise a rock into the air with magic.

"Don't forget to clean out the stable," said Sidesaddle.

"I don't want to," said Jack, stamping his foot angrily. "I came here to learn magic not to clean out stables!"

Sidesaddle looked at him over his glasses, his eyes flashing. For a moment Jack wondered if he had gone too far. After all, his master was a wizard, and everyone knew that annoying a wizard could be dangerous. Then the old man sighed and sat down, pointing to a log on which Jack took a seat as well.

"You may think such work is not important young Jack," said the wizard seriously. "But let me tell you, that horse is no ordinary horse and it deserves looking after. Let me tell you the story...."

*************************   ***********************

There was once a king who had three sons. One day they went hunting in some woods, and there the youngest prince became separated from his brothers. They searched for him all day, but in the end were forced to return home without him.

The prince wandered through the forest for four days, living on roots and berries. Then he came to a great house hidden among the trees. The door stood wide open, so the prince went inside and looked around. The house was full of wonderful things, but there was no sign of anyone there at all.

The prince wandered through the empty rooms until he came to a great hall. And there was a table spread with fine food and wine. The prince sat down and ate and drank his fill. As soon as he was finished the table and all the food left uneaten vanished away.

This astonished the prince, but at that moment an old man entered the room

"What are you doing in my house?" he demanded.

"Sir, forgive me, "said the prince. "I got lost in the wood and have been wandering for days. If you would take me into your service I will serve you faithfully."

"Very well," said the old man. "You may serve me. I shall pay you a single gold coin every week. To earn that you must keep the stove in the cellar always lit, and care for the black horse that is in my stable. If you do this there will be food on the table every day and you may eat your fill. Do you agree to this?"

The prince agreed, and so he came to work for the old man, who came and went on mysterious errands so that the prince seldom saw him.

One day he let the fire in the stove almost die out. The old man came rushing in at the last moment, and threw a log onto the fire. "Be more careful," he cried angrily, "If that fire ever goes out you will suffer the consequences."

THE MAGICIAN'S HORSE

And so the prince lived in the old man's house for a year and served him faithfully. But he never forgot that he was not really a servant and often thought of his brothers and wondered what they were doing.

Then one day, as he was sitting rather sadly in the stable, he suddenly heard a voice speaking to him. It was the black horse.

"Come into my stall' it said. "I have much to tell you."

The prince was astonished. "You can talk!" he cried.

"Of course' said the horse, "I am a magician's horse after all. Oh yes, didn't you know the old man for whom you work is a magician?"

The prince confessed that he did not.

"Well' said the horse, "here is what you must do. Fetch my saddle and bridle from that cupboard. Next to them you will find a bottle. The salve within it will make your hair shine like pure gold."

The prince did as he was told and sure enough his hair looked just like gold.

"Now," said the magician's horse, "gather as much wood as you can and fill the stove right to the top."

The prince hurried to obey. The stove grew hotter and hotter, and soon flames shot out of it and set fire to the magician's house. The prince hastened back to the stable.

"We do not have long," the horse declared. "Soon the magician will be back. Look in the cupboard again and you will find three things: a mirror, a brush and a whip. Bring them to me. But hurry, for we must be gone."

The prince brought the mirror, the brush and the whip and then he mounted on the black horse's back and they rode off as fast as the wind.

Before they had gone far the horse's keen ears heard the sounds of pursuit.

"Look behind you!" he cried. "What can you see?"

"There is a cloud, like smoke or dust, on the horizon' said the Prince.

"That will be the magician," said the horse, and he galloped even faster.

After a while the horse said again, "Look over your shoulder and tell me what you see."

The prince did so. The cloud of dust was much nearer.

"Quickly," said the horse, "throw the mirror behind us!"

The Prince took out the mirror and threw it in the road. There it grew suddenly large.

Presently the magician came along, and his horse put its foot on the mirror. The glass gave way with a crack and the horse fell and hurt itself so badly that the magician was forced to walk home, leading his mount.

The Prince meanwhile rode on as fast as he could.

But soon the black horse's ears began to twitch.

"Look behind you," he said. "Tell me what you see."

The Prince looked.

"I see a cloud of smoke and a tongue of flame."

"That is my master," said the horse. "Be quick and throw the brush behind you."

The Prince did as he was told and as soon as the brush touched the ground it became a thick and tangled forest. When the magician arrived on a new horse, he could not get through and was forced to go around the forest.

If the magician had been angry before, now he was furious. He rode so fast that soon he saw the Prince in the distance. But the black horse had heard him coming.

"Look behind you," he said to the Prince. "What do you see?"

"I see a tongue of fire coming closer."

"Then you must throw down the whip' said the horse.

The Prince did as he was bidden, and as soon as the whip touched the ground it turned into a deep river.

The magician rode up to the edge of the river and urged his mount into it.

The water rose higher and higher, until finally it came up so high that it put out the magic fire that was the source of the magician's power. The flame went out with a fizz and the magician vanished, never to be seen again.

The black horse slowed to a halt. "We are safe now," it said.

They rode on for a little way until they came to a lake.

"See that willow tree?" said the horse. "Gather a branch from it and strike the ground just over there."

The Prince did so and a vaulted archway sprang up out of the earth. The Prince led the horse through it and found himself in a huge hall.

"I will stay here for awhile," said the horse, "But if you want to improve your fortune, you must go on alone until you come to a garden. Within it is a king's palace. Go there and ask to be taken into the king's service. But first of all hide your golden hair under a hat. Trust me, and you will go far. But be sure you do not forget me."

So the prince took his leave of the black horse and went on as he had been instructed. Soon he found himself in a wonderful garden. There he saw the walls and towers of the king's palace.

At the gate he met the royal gardener.

"What do you want?" asked the man.

"I want to take service with the king."

"Then you can work for me," said the gardener. "I need someone to sweep the paths and weed the flowerbeds. If you do that you will get a silver penny a day, somewhere to sleep and food every day."

So the prince started working in the king's garden. Every day he swept the leaves and pulled up the weeds. And every day he took half the food he was given to the black horse.

One day when they were together after the prince had finished his work the black horse addressed him, "Tomorrow a number of princes and great lords are coming to the king's castle to woo his three beautiful daughters. They will all stand in a row, and when the three princesses come out they will each be carrying a diamond apple. They will throw these down and whichever prince's feet they roll to will be that princess's husband. See to it that you are near at hand when this happens. The youngest princess's apple will fall near to you. Pick it up quickly and put it in your pocket. After that we shall see."

So the prince did as the horse told him. When the royal suitors were gathered out came the three princesses—and the youngest was indeed the fairest of them all. Her apple rolled further than all the rest, and came to the feet of the gardener's boy, who picked it up and put it in his pocket. As he did so the hat covering his hair slipped, and the princess caught a glimpse of his bright golden hair.

"There is more to this young man than there seems to be," she thought. And as she looked at him she felt her heart beat faster.

THE MAGICIAN'S HORSE

The king was most unhappy about this turn of events. But he had made it a decree that whoever caught the apples would marry that princess. So the next day there were three weddings celebrated, and when the two older princesses married their noble lords, the youngest married the gardener's boy, and went home with him to the little hut where he lived.

Next day something happened which put everything else out of the king's head. News came that a neighbouring kingdom had declared war. The king prepared for battle at once, and next day he rode out with the two husbands of his eldest daughters riding at his side. But he was so ashamed of the gardener's boy that he would not even give him a horse to ride with them.

As soon as the army had departed the prince went to where the black horse was stabled. When he told the horse what had happened the noble beast said at once, "I will carry you to the battle. Fetch my saddle. Also, look in the next room and you will find armour and a sword which you may carry."

Thus, the prince rode forth looking as fine as any noble lord. When he reached the battlefield the king's side was losing. But, when the prince joined in, he fought so bravely that the tide turned. The great black horse carried him everywhere, and he hewed left and right with his shining sword. Everyone thought he was a great hero who had come to help them, but no one recognised the poor gardener's boy.

Towards the end of the battle the prince received a wound in the leg. When the king saw this he tied up the wound with his own scarf, embroidered with crowns and his royal name. He tried to get the prince to climb onto a litter and be carried home, but the hero climbed onto the back of the black horse which then mounted into the sky and flew away with him!

The prince was soon home, and when he had seen that the black horse was safely stabled, he lay down on his bed and fell into an exhausted sleep. There the princess found him. Noticing the blood soaked scarf around his leg she looked more closely and saw the king's name upon it. Hearing the victorious army returning, she hurried to fetch her father. When he saw his scarf on the prince's leg he realised at once what had happened.

Everyone was overjoyed to learn that the hero of the battle was really a prince, and furthermore that he was married to their own princess! The prince told them the whole story, and the black horse was fetched and given a place in the royal stable. After that the prince and princess lived long and happily. The prince often went to visit the magical horse, and they had many more adventures together and remained good friends for the rest of their lives.

**************************   ************************

As Sidesaddle fell silent Jack sat with his mouth open. "You mean," he said at last, "that the horse I take apples to and whose stable I clean out is that horse...?"

Sidesaddle looked at him with just a hint of a smile. "That is for you to find out, young Jack. But I'd hurry up and get the work done if I were you."

THE WIZARD KING

(A Story from France)

"What can you tell me about Fairies?" Jack asked the wizard one day. Sidesaddle put down the rather interesting object he had just created out of thin air and looked into the distance. "Well," he said at last, "they can be a funny lot. Tricky. Not always to be trusted. There has been not much liking between Wizards and Fairies over the centuries. But I have to admit they can be helpful at times. There's a story I heard about a not very nice wizard who was defeated by Fairy magic. Would you like to hear it?"

"Please," said Jack, settling down in his chair by the fire.

"Very well," said Sidesaddle, and began to speak....

************************** ************************

There was once a king who was also a very powerful wizard. When it came time for him to marry he chose a wife who was as clever as she was beautiful, and he loved her greatly.

Soon she gave birth to a beautiful child, a boy, who was the apple of both his father's and his mother's eyes.

But the queen had a secret. As a child, she had been entrusted to the care of a Fairy Godmother, who watched over her ever after. She could not tell the Wizard King about this, because, as everyone knows, there has always been great rivalry

41

between Fairies and Wizards, and the Queen did not want to make her husband angry.

So, when the baby was but a few weeks old, she took him in secret to visit the Fairy, who blessed him with two gifts: the power of pleasing everyone he met, and the power of learning everything he was taught with the greatest ease.

The little prince grew into a handsome young man, as clever as he was popular.

Then, when he was nineteen years old, his mother, the Queen, died quite suddenly.

The prince was heartbroken. But his grief was nothing to that of his father. The Wizard King was inconsolable. Everywhere he looked he saw things that reminded him of the Queen.

And so, he decided to travel to distant lands, so that he might see nothing but new and unfamiliar things.

Changing himself into an eagle, he flew far and wide over land and sea.

Then, one day, he came to a most wonderful country where the sun always seemed to shine and the scent of jasmine filled the air.

The Wizard King flew down and settled in the topmost branches of a tall tree. All around him stretched the most beautiful gardens filled with rare flowers and fountains that shot great jets of silvery water into the air.

There, floating on the surface of an artificial lake, was a golden barge, and in the barge sat the most beautiful princess the Wizard King had ever seen.

At once he fell in love with her, and without a further thought he flew down in his eagle's form, and gripping her in his huge talons, carried her off.

THE WIZARD KING

The princess cried and cried and struggled and struggled, but the Wizard King flew onward until he was in sight of his own land. There he landed in the midst of a flowery meadow and turned himself back into his own shape.

"Do not weep, I beg you," he said. "I have brought you here to be my queen and to rule over my kingdom with me. My only wish is to make you happy."

But the Princess began to weep all the harder. "If you truly want to make me happy," she cried, "take me home."

The Wizard King only looked at her sadly and said, "I shall care for you always. You will be happy in time."

Then he took on the form of an eagle again and carried the Princess to a place close to his own palace. There, with his magic, he made a wonderful dwelling for her, a tower of ivory and glass, beautifully furnished. He summoned maidens to wait upon her, and a wonderful talking parrot to entertain her, and the finest food that was ever seen. Then he left her, for in his heart he believed that, in time, she would grow to love him.

Every day the Wizard King visited the Princess, bringing her gifts and speaking kind and gentle words to her. But there were no doors in the tower, and the Princess knew that she was a prisoner. So she felt only hatred for the Wizard King, and longed to be set free.

At first the king was patient, but as time passed and the Princess remained as cold and sad as the day he had brought her home, he began to grow suspicious.

"Perhaps," he thought, "she has seen my son, who is so handsome and accomplished she must have fallen in love with him."

So the Wizard King decided to send his son away, to travel and learn more of the world outside his father's kingdom.

The Prince set out joyously, for he loved to see new places. He travelled through many kingdoms, until he came to the very one from which the Wizard King had stolen the Princess. The King and Queen of that land made him most welcome, but they could not hide the sorrow they felt at the loss of their beloved daughter.

Then one day when the Prince was visiting the Queen in her own rooms, he saw a portrait hanging on the wall. At once he asked who the beautiful girl in the picture was, and with tears in her eyes the Queen told him it was the Princess who had been carried off by a great eagle.

The Prince swore that he would not rest until he had found the lost Princess—for if the truth were known he was head over heels in love with her, even though he had never seen her in his own country, so secretive was his father, the Wizard King. The Queen swore that if he succeeded he should get her daughter in marriage, and half the kingdom as well.

The Prince set out, carrying with him a miniature portrait of the Princess. He went straight to the Fairy under whose protection his mother had placed him.

She listened to the Prince's story and went to consult her magic books.

When she came back she said, "It was your own father who carried off the Princess. She is nearby, imprisoned in a tower, surrounded by a magical mist. It will be very hard to get through."

"What can I do?" asked the Prince.

The Fairy thought for a while, then she said, "The Princess

has a wonderful talking parrot in her tower. It is the only thing, except for the Wizard King, which is allowed to come and go as it pleases. It often flies this way. I will catch it and use my magic to turn you into the shape of the Parrot. That way you can visit the Princess and no one will ever know."

Everything turned out as the Fairy planned. She caught the parrot next time it left the tower and shut it in a golden cage. Then the Prince, in the shape of the bird, flew through the magical mist and entered the tower.

The Princess was every bit as beautiful as her portrait. The Prince was so dazzled that he could not speak, and the Princess became quite worried, for she loved the Parrot dearly.

She took the bird in her arms and cradled it, stroking its head and wings.

This made the prince very happy indeed.

Then the Wizard King came in and the Prince saw at once how much the Princess hated him. As soon as he had gone—having once again failed to persuade the Princess to like him even a little—the Prince spoke.

"My lady, don't be afraid. I am here to help you."

"What can you do, dear Parrot?" cried the Princess in astonishment.

"I am not really the parrot' said the Prince. "I have come from your mother, the Queen." And he took from beneath one wing the miniature portrait the Queen had given him.

When she saw it, the Princess burst out crying again.

"Please don't weep," said the Prince. He told her of the Fairy and how she had promised to help them. Then he asked if he might take his own shape again.

Drying her tears the Princess said yes. The Parrot pulled

one feather from its wing, and there stood the Prince in human form. The Princess thought she had never seen a more handsome person, and she fell in love with him at once.

Meanwhile, the Fairy prepared a magical chariot, to which she harnessed two mighty eagles. Then she took the Parrot in the golden cage and commanded the bird to take them to the Princess.

Thus they passed through the mist quite easily and hovered outside the Princess's window. The Prince and Princess looked out and saw her, and the Princess was very happy to see her Parrot again. Together they climbed out of the window and got into the chariot. Then the Fairy, who was riding on the back of one of the eagles, commanded the great birds to fly back through the mist to the Princess's own country.

Meanwhile, the Wizard King dreamed that the Princess was being carried off. When he woke he went straight to the magic tower, and sure enough the Princess was gone. The Wizard King was furious. He went to consult his magic books, and very quickly found what had happened.

Raging, he turned himself into a fearsome monster and set off in pursuit. But the Fairy sent a powerful wind to slow him down so that the Prince and Princess arrived safely at the Princess' home.

The King and Queen greeted them with delight and thankfulness, but the Fairy warned them that the Wizard King would soon be there.

"The only way to stop him killing you both is to get married at once," the Fairy said.

The Prince and Princess were more than willing, and the king and Queen agreed, a wedding was quickly celebrated. But just as the ceremony was ending, the Wizard King arrived.

He was so angry at the sight of the Prince and Princess happy together, that he changed back into his human shape and tried to sprinkle some black liquid over the bride and groom.

If it had touched them they would have died instantly, but luckily for them the Fairy made a magical wind that blew the liquid all over the Wizard King instead.

He fell down in a heap at once, unable to move hand or foot. While he was unconscious the Princess' father ordered him to be carried away and put in prison.

Now it is well known that wizards lose all their power when they are imprisoned. The Wizard King was thus completely helpless, and felt very sorry for himself. The Prince took pity on his father and pleaded with the King to set him free. In his gratitude the King agreed, and as soon as the doors of the prison were opened, the Wizard King flew out in the shape of a strange bird.

With a cry he flew off, vowing never to see his son again.

After that everything was very peaceful. The Prince and Princess settled down together, and in time they ruled the kingdom wisely. They were helped by the Fairy, who was persuaded to settle in that land, and who sent for all her books and built a great palace for herself next to that of the Prince and Princess.

**************************   ************************

"Hmmm...," said Jack, as the wizard finished his story. "That's another not very nice wizard."

"It's like I said before," answered Sidesaddle. "If you let power go to your head you get very proud and think you are the most important person in the world. That's what the Wizard King thought, but as you see it didn't do him any good in the end."

"But how do you stop that from happening?" asked Jack.

"A lot depends on the person," answered the wizard thoughtfully. "Whenever I take a new apprentice I try to choose one who won't forget how fortunate they are to be alive and able to use magic."

Jack looked at him. "Am I like that?" he asked.

"That depends," said Sidesaddle. "I haven't decided yet."

THE BOY MAGICIAN

(Native American)

One day Jack and the Wizard went out to collect certain herbs Sidesaddle needed for a potion. Eventually they came to a small lake. It was a hot day and Jack thought how wonderful it would be to jump into the cool water and bathe, but the Wizard (who always seemed to know what he was thinking) stopped him.

"Not every bit of calm water is safe," he said.

"But it looks so lovely and cold," said Jack.

"That may be so," said the Wizard, "but you never know what lies beneath the water." Seeing Jack's look of longing, the Wizard sat down under a tree. "Let me tell you a story about a boy who found out just how dangerous still pools of water can be," he said.

**************************   ************************

In the heart of a wilderness there once lived an old woman and her young grandson. Both the boy's parents were dead, but from his father he had inherited some small skill in magic, so that his grandmother used to call him "my young magician."

They were happy enough in their life together. By day the old woman would be busy with cooking and cleaning, while the young boy went hunting to catch food for their table.

Often the Grandmother would talk about the time when the

boy would be ready to go out into the world.

"Always go to the East," she would say. "Never go to the West, for that way lies danger."

But no matter how often the boy asked her, she would never say what kind of danger lay to the West. And as he grew older and stronger the boy thought that one day he would have to go and find out for himself.

One day the old woman said again, "Never go to the West." But this time the boy—who was really a young man now—would not rest until he had an answer from her. At last, reluctantly, she said, "There is a creature out there. A terrible creature. It wants to do harm to everyone who sees it. If you were to go near it we should both be killed."

More than that she would not say, but her words only made the young man want to go and find out about this creature. He trusted his strength and skill and his knowledge of magic to keep both himself and his grandmother safe.

And so, when he set out next morning to go hunting, as soon as he was out of sight of his Grandmother's lodge he turned West.

All day he travelled and saw nothing. Then he came to the edge of a lake, where he decided to rest. He had not been there long when he suddenly heard a strange voice.

"I see you," said the voice.

The boy looked all around him, and at the sky, but he could see no one."

"Where are you?" he asked.

"Where you cannot see me," answered the voice. Then it said, "I am going to send a hurricane. It will smash your grandmother's house to pieces. How do you like that?"

THE BOY MAGICIAN

"Why, thank you," said the boy. "We are always needing firewood. Now we shall have plenty."

"Go home," said the voice. "I dare say you won't like it that much."

So the boy hurried home. When he was almost in sight of the lodge a great wind blew up from nowhere. It rooted trees out of the ground and threw rocks about as though they were pebbles. The boy's grandmother looked out and saw him coming.

"Quickly," she cried, "get inside before you are killed."

As soon as he was inside the old woman began to scold him.

"You have been to the West," she said. "Now we are both going to die."

"Don't worry grandmother," said the boy. "I shall use my magic to turn the walls of the lodge to stone."

He spoke some magic words and though the hurricane blew as strongly as it could, it could not even move the stone lodge. When it had blow itself out the old woman and the boy went outside and found enough firewood to last them for a month.

Next day the boy was ready to go to the West again. But his Grandmother begged and pleaded with him until he promised to go East instead. He set out that way, but soon his feet turned West again and soon he was back at the lake.

He looked all around and could see nothing.

Then he heard the strange voice again.

"I'm going to send a great storm of hail to destroy your grandmother's lodge. What do you think of that?"

"I should like that," said the boy. "I need some new spears."

"Go home then," said the voice, "but I don't think you'll be so pleased."

The boy hurried home, and just as he was nearing his Grandmother's lodge the sky got very dark. Huge hailstones the size of boulders began to fall out of the sky.

The boy ran as fast as he could and got safely into the lodge where his Grandmother waited.

"Now we shall surely die," the old woman cried.

But once again the boy used his magic and turned the walls of the lodge to stone. The hailstones banged and rattled against them, bouncing off harmlessly.

When the storm was over the boy came out of the lodge and saw that there were dozens of sharp, glittering spearheads sticking in the ground.

He ran to get poles to fit them to. But when he returned the spearheads had vanished.

"Where are all my beautiful spears?" he demanded.

"They have all melted away," said his Grandmother. "They were only made of ice."

The boy was very disappointed. He began to wonder how he could get back on the owner of the voice.

"Don't be so foolish," his Grandmother said. "Take my advice and leave well enough alone."

But the boy was determined to be avenged. He took a certain stone that was full of magic and hung it around his neck on a thong. Then he set off back to the lake.

This time he went as stealthily as he could, and when he arrived at the lake he crouched down behind a big rock and looked at every inch of the place.

At first he saw nothing, then as he was watching he saw a horrible head pop up out of the middle of the lake. It had a face not only on the front, but on the sides and back as well. Eight eyes, eight ears, four noses, four mouths.

"I see you," cried the youth. Then he said, "How would you like it if this lake dried up?"

"Nonsense' said the ugly head, speaking out of all four of its mouths, "That could never happen."

"Go home and see," shouted the boy, imitating the head. Then he took the stone from around his neck and threw it up into the air. As it went it got bigger, and when it fell in the lake it made a great splash.

At once the water began to boil and bubble, and the head made a great roaring sound.

The boy ran away home as fast as he could and told his Grandmother what had happened.

"It's no good," she said. "Others have tried to kill him, but they have all died."

Nonetheless the boy decided to go back to the lake next day. When he arrived he found the lake had boiled away entirely, and that all the creatures in it were dead—except for a big green frog that was hopping weakly about in the middle.

The boy looked at it and knew that this was what the creature that had plagued him was really like.

He took a big stick and went to kill it.

"Please spare me," cried the frog in a little voice, not at all like the one it had used to terrify so many people.

But the boy thought of all those who had been killed by the monster, and he struck the frog with his stick and killed it. Then he went home and told his Grandmother all that had happened.

After that they lived in peace, and now the old woman called her grandson, "My great big magician," because of the good use to which he had put his magic.

***************************   *************************

"So the creature wasn't really as big and terrible as everyone thought," said Jack.

"Well, it was strong enough to kill people," said Sidesaddle. But it's often the way, Jack, that things that appear big and frightening are really cowards at heart."

"Well I'm glad the monster got killed," said Jack, fiercely. He looked at the still lake and asked, "It wasn't this lake, was it?"

The wizard stood up, shaking the dust off his cloak. "I don't think so," he said with a smile. "Probably not."

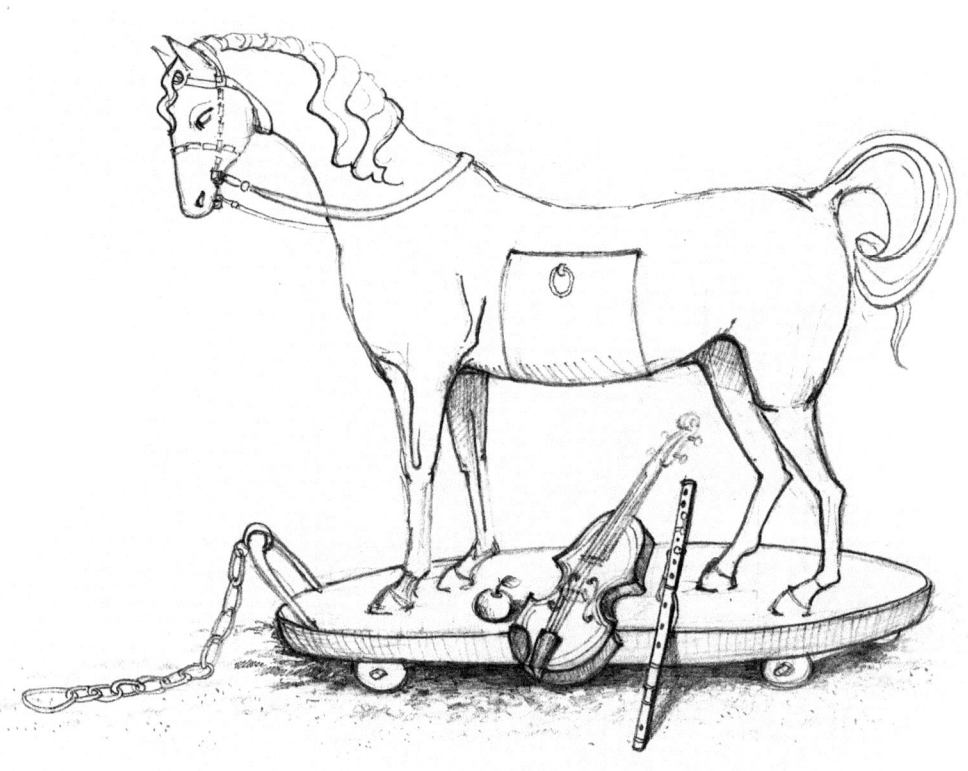

POMME AND PEEL

(A Story from Italy)

"I've been thinking," said Jack one day, when he and Sidesaddle had spent several hours revising Jack's spell-work. "Sometimes magic can really get you in trouble."

"That's very true," said Sidesaddle. "But as long as you don't jump to conclusions and fire off spells without thinking, it can do a lot of good as well."

"Do you know any stories about that?" asked Jack.

"Well, as a matter of fact I do," answered his master. "I knew a wizard once who made life very difficult for several people, but in the end he realised he was wrong...."

Jack leaned forward eagerly as the old wizard began...

*************************   ***********************

There was once a noble lord and his lady who longed to have a son, but no matter how much they wished they were unlucky, and so the lord decided to visit a certain wizard he knew of to ask for his help.

The wizard gave him an apple. "Give this to your wife to eat "he said, "and you will soon have a fine son."

The Lord took the apple home and told his wife what the wizard had said.

The Lady was delighted and sent for her maid to peel the apple. The maid did so, but instead of throwing the peel away, she ate it.

Which is why, nine months later, a son was born to the lady and to the maidservant, on the same day and at the same time. The Lord looked at them both and saw that they were as alike as alike, save that the maid's child had skin as red and bright as the sun, while his own wife's child had skin as white as the pulp of an apple. And so he named them Pome and Peel, and decided to bring them both up as his own sons.

And so the two boys grew to manhood like brothers. Then one day they heard about a wizard's daughter, who was said to be more beautiful than the morning star. But no one had ever seen her because the wizard protected her and never allowed her to go out of his house.

"How can we get to see this wonderful girl?" said Pome.

"I have an idea," said Peel. "Let's build a horse of bronze and hide inside it."

So that is what they did. They took the bronze horse to the wizard's house and climbed inside its hollow belly with a violin and a flute. Then they began to play.

The wizard looked out of his window and saw the marvellous creature which seemed to be making music all on its own. Immediately the wizard went out and brought the bronze horse inside.

He called to his daughter, "Come and see what I have found for you."

The maiden came from her room to look at the horse and was quite delighted. She sat down to listen to the music while the wizard went about his own business.

POMME AND PEEL

But as soon as the wizard had gone, out jumped Pome and Peel.

The wizard's daughter was frightened at first, but Pome said, "Don't be afraid. We won't hurt you. We heard all about your beauty and we wanted to see for ourselves." And Peel said, "If you like we can go away, but if you like our music we can keep playing for a while. Then we'll go and no one need ever know we were here."

The wizard's daughter smiled shyly and asked them to play some more for her. And, by the time they had spent several hours together, she did not want them to go at all. Indeed, she had fallen in love with Pome, and when he—who felt the same way about her as she about him—suggested that she come with them, she agreed at once.

They all got inside the bronze horse and rolled it outside the wizard's house and so escaped entirely unseen.

When the wizard came home he looked high and low for his daughter. When he could find so sign of her he consulted his magic books and quickly learned what had happened.

The wizard was beside himself with rage. He rushed upstairs, leaned out of the window and screamed three curses after his daughter.

This is what they were:

First: that she should see three horses, one red, one white and one black. Then, since she loved horses more than anything, she would jump on the back of the white one, which would run off with her and throw her off over a cliff onto some rocks.

Second: that she should see three dogs, one red, one white, one black, and that she should pick up the black dog, which would tear out her throat.

Third: that on the first night she spent with her husband, a great snake should come in through the window of their room and destroy them both.

Now it happened that three fairies were passing below the window at that moment, and so they heard everything. Later on that night they stopped at an inn, and there they saw the wizard's daughter, with Pome and Peel, sleeping beside the fire.

"My goodness' said one of the fairies, "they wouldn't sleep so soundly if they knew what was in store for them."

Now Peel wasn't actually asleep at all, and so he overheard everything the three fairies said.

First they talked about the three horses.

"If only someone was there when it happened, he could cut off the white horse's head. Then everything would be all right," said the first fairy.

"And if only someone was there when she meets the dogs he could cut off the black one's head. Then that would be all right' said the second fairy.

"And if only someone were there when the snake comes through the window, he could cut off its head, then everything would be all right' said the third fairy.

"Except," said the first fairy, "if anyone were to breath a word about this, they would turn to stone at once."

Peel lay quiet and thought about all he had heard. He knew everything that was going to happen to Pome and the wizard's daughter, but he did not dare speak of it for fear of turning to stone. Then he thought how much he loved his brother and how fair the wizard's daughter was, and he decided to do what he could to help.

Next morning they set out along the way. Pome had already

sent word home to his father, and in a while they met with a messenger who had brought three horses with him for them to ride. The wizard's daughter immediately jumped on the back of the white horse, but Peel drew his sword and with one blow cut off its head.

"What are you doing? Have you gone mad?" cried the wizard's daughter.

Peel shook his head. "I cannot tell you," he said.

Then the wizard's daughter turned to Pome. "Your brother has an evil heart. I do not want to travel any further with him."

But Peel swore that he had acted in a moment of madness, and begged her to forgive him.

They rode on until they came in sight of Pome and Peel's house. The three little dogs ran out to greet them, one red, one white, and one black. The wizard's daughter bent to pick up the black one, but Peel drew his sword and cut off its head with a single blow.

"Monster!" cried the wizard's daughter. "Why are you so cruel?"

Again Peel said nothing. Then Pome's parents came out and did their best to smooth things over. They persuaded the wizard's daughter that Peel must have been temporarily mad. They all went inside and the wedding of Pome and the wizard's daughter was celebrated.

But during the great feast that followed Peel hardly said a word to anyone. To everyone who asked he said that he felt fine, and that nothing was the matter. Then he excused himself and went off to bed early.

But instead of going to his own room, he went into the

bridal chamber and hid under the bed. Soon the couple arrived and got into bed. When they were asleep Peel crept out and drew his sword. In a little while the window opened and in slithered a huge snake. With a cry Peel leapt upon it and cut off its head with a single blow.

Woken by the noise Pome and his bride sat up in bed and saw Peel with his drawn sword. But the snake had vanished the moment its head was cut off, so they thought that he was about to attack them.

"Call the guards!" shouted Pome, while the wizard's daughter cried out that she had forgiven Peel twice now but this time he should be put in prison and then executed.

So Peel was seized and thrown into a dungeon to await death. Realising that he was doomed anyway, he sent a message to the wizard's daughter, begging her to visit him in prison.

Reluctantly, she came. Peel looked at her sadly.

"Do you remember," he said, "how when we were on the way here we stopped at an inn to rest."

"Of course," said the Princess

"Well, while you and Pome were asleep three fairies came in. I overheard them talking, and they said that your father had placed three curses upon you. The first was that when you saw three horses you would get on the white one and that it would cause your death. But if someone were to cut its head off then everything would be well. Except that, if anyone breathed a word of this they would turn to stone."

Even as he said this Peel's feet and legs turned to marble.

"Stop!" cried the wizard's daughter.

But Peel said, "I am doomed anyway." And he old her about the curse of the three dogs.

POMME AND PEEL

As he spoke his body turned to marble up to the neck

"I understand. I forgive you," cried the wizard's daughter. "Please don't say any more!"

But Peel, speaking with difficulty, told her of the snake.

As he did so, he fell silent, and in his place stood a marble statue.

"Alas!" said the wizard's daughter, "Poor Peel, what have I done!"

Then she thought, "There is only one person who can undo this terrible wrong, and that is my father." And she took pen and ink and paper and wrote a letter to him, begging his forgiveness and asking him to come to her as quickly as possible.

When he got her letter the wizard came at once, for indeed he loved his daughter more than anything.

As soon as he arrived the wizard's daughter ran straight to him and flung her arms about his neck.

"O Father," she said, "I am sorry for making you angry. But I really do love Pome and we are very happy."

"Well..." said her father.

"There is only one thing that makes me sad," and she took him to the statue of Peel.

"This good youth was only trying to help. Please will you bring him back to life?"

The wizard sighed. "Very well," he said, "I will do this for you."

He took a phial of liquid from a pocket in his robes and let fall a little of it onto the statue. At once Peel sprang up alive again, and there was great rejoicing. And when the wizard saw Pome and Peel together he recognised them as the children of the Lord and Lady he had helped long ago by giving them a magic apple.

Then he was truly sorry for all that he had done, and thereafter everyone lived very happily for the rest of their days.

**************************   ************************

"So even wizards, who must be the cleverest people in the world, can get things wrong," said Jack

"Well, first of all we are not really that much cleverer than anyone," answered Sidesaddle. "The thing about being a wizard is to remember that you should always do good with your magic. If you do that you won't go far wrong."

"But suppose you see someone doing something horrible," said Jack. "It's ok then to use your magic to stop them, isn't it?"

The old wizard sighed. "So many of my apprentices have asked me that," he said. "The truth is, it is never good to hurt people with your magic. You might turn someone into some thing else for a while, but even then you have to think of the consequences. If the wizard in my story had stopped to think, Peel would not have had to do those terrible things and get turned to stone."

"But how do you know what's right?" asked Jack.

"That's more difficult to answer than any spell," said Sidesaddle. "In the end, only your heart can tell you what's right. Listen to what your heart tells you, young Jack, and you won't go far wrong."

THREE MAGICIANS

(Ghana)

Jack and Sidesaddle were sitting in the Wizard's study.

"I've been with you for ages now," said Jack, "and you've still not told me what makes a good wizard."

"Ah..." said Sidesaddle, looking off into the distance.

After a minute he said:

****************************   ************************

One day three magicians came to a river that was swollen by floods.

"How shall we cross?" they asked each other.

"Let's use our magic," said one, and he took a piece of rope from his pocket and threw one end of it across the river. At once it became a bridge and the magician walked across to the other side. There the bridge became a piece of rope again and he rolled it up and put it away.

"You see, my magic is the strongest!" he said.

"Well, we'll see about that," said the second magician.

He took a small bottle out of his pocket and conjured all the water into it. Then he strolled across the dry riverbed. On the other side he opened the bottle and all the water flowed back out.

"You see, it's really my magic which is the strongest." he said.

The third magician said nothing. He waved his hands and produced a ball of fire that went into the water and turned it all to steam.

Then he walked across to the other side, and once there withdrew the ball of fire so that the steam became water again.

"You are both wrong," he said. "My magic is by far the strongest."

*************************   *************************

"Which one was right?" said Sidesaddle. "Can you decide, Jack?"

"Well...?" said Jack, thinking furiously.

"Mull it over," said the Wizard with a smile. "Whatever answer you come up with, it's your own and no one else's. That's what makes a good Wizard."

Years later, when Jack became a famous wizard in his own

right, applying all the wisdom he had learned from his teacher, he felt one afternoon as he was tending the dragon eggs that it was time to take on an apprentice. The next day, he let it be known the position was open. The moment he did so, because he was a wizard, he knew that a young boy named Tom would show up at his door in three days time.

Which is exactly what happened.

The first evening they were together, Tom asked him, "What does it mean to be a wizard?" Jack thought for a moment, remembering his first evening with Sidesaddle. Finally, levitating a log onto the fire in the fireplace, he smoothed out his wizard's robe and said, "Let me tell you a story...."

NOTES

1: The Story Of Emrys. This story makes its first recorded appearance in *The History of The Kings of Britain* by Geoffrey of Monmouth, written in the 12th century. It was the first book to tell the story of King Arthur from birth to death, and it became a best seller of the time. The story of Merlin was originally attached to an older figure called Emrys or Ambrosius. After the publication of Geoffrey's book it became inseparably linked with the myths of Arthur.

2: The Wizard Who Got Sick. This wonderful story from Armenia was told by a peasant woman named Gyuli Avagian in 1950, though it has probably been circulating for a lot longer than this. The idea of the wizard who goes about doing good deeds is an interesting variant on the more negative side of wizardry, which is found in many folk-stories. In the original version it was a baby that the wizard ate and then brought back to life next day. I changed this as the idea was that the couple should give up something of importance, and when you have only one cow killing it is a big thing.

3: Magic. Versions of this story are to be found all over the world. I have found English, French, German and Swiss versions, but none as good or varied as this Russian tale, which appears in a number of collections. The theme of the chase and the transformations of the wizard and his apprentice appear in a variant form in the Welsh tale of "Taliesin."

4: The Magician's Horse. This story from modern day Greece still manages to preserve some elements of its Classical heritage. The story of the three princesses with their diamond apples probably goes back to the Judgment of Paris, which caused the Trojan War to begin when an unfortunate prince gave the prize for beauty to the mortal Helen of Troy rather than the Goddess Aphrodite. Talking horses are a common feature of folk-tales, and I rather liked that it was the horse that is the hero here, rather than the magician himself.

5: The Wizard King. I love the way this story preserves the age-old rivalry between the Fairy people, who inherit their magic, and the wizards, who learn their magic in school. There is also a marvelously circular aspect to the tale, with everything working out satisfactorily at the end through a series of coincidences and the intervention of a magical bird. I first read it in one of the great collections of Fairy tales made by Andrew Lang in the 19th century. Lang gives his source as the *Cabinet de Fees* (The Fairy Box), one of the most famous collections of French folk-tales.

6: The Boy Magician. Versions of this Native American story are told all over the United States. I particularly liked this one, which I heard while visiting friends in New Mexico. There it belongs to the Hopi people, whose traditions are still very much alive today.

NOTES

7: Pome and Peel. This story combines lots of wonderful elements: the magical birth of the two heroes, the trick by which they get into the magician's house, the triple curse and the Fairy helpers who happen to be in the right place at the right time, and the final sacrifice of Peel (who get's a pretty raw deal all round like most younger brothers) who is still saved at the last minute. It comes from the Umbrian region of Italy, where stories of resourceful heroes and heroines are still told to this day, where the concept of working magic is less strange than it seems to other Europeans.

8: Three Magicians. This brief tale from Africa seems to sum up everything there is to say about being a magician and working magic. I wanted to end with it because it leaves young Jack, the apprentice wizard, at exactly the point where he has to learn to think for himself, which is what each of the stories he heard helps him to do.

About the Artist

Deva Berg is a long-time resident of Los Angeles, CA. She is the author of *A Tail of Two Sisters* and artist for Dorothy Maclean's *Seeds of Inspirations* as well as David Spangler's *Manifestation* and *Soul's Oracle* card decks. When not illustrating or painting, she works as a designer and construction specialist at W3 Architects Inc., a firm specializing in passive solar, resource conserving design. She is married and has a wonderful daughter, Xyla Mae.

About the Publisher

Starseed Books is an imprimatur of Lorian Press LLC. Starseed Books specializes in fiction but also publishes biographies, books by JM Greer for the Ancient Order of Druids in America and other material.

Starseed Books
Attn: Jeremy Berg
6592 Peninsula Dr
Traverse City, MI 49686

www.lorianpress.com